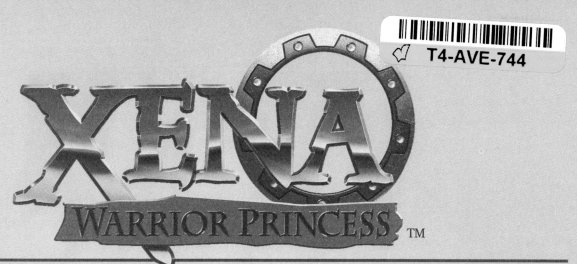

QUEEN OF THE AMAZONS

By Kerry Milliron

Based on the Universal television series created by John Schulian and Robert Tapert

Adapted from the episode "Hooves and Harlots," teleplay by Steven L. Sears

Copyright © 1996 by MCA Publishing Rights, a division of MCA, Inc.
All rights reserved under International and Pan-American Copyright Conventions. Published in the United States by Random House, Inc., New York, and simultaneously in Canada by Random House of Canada Limited, Toronto
http://www.randomhouse.com/
Library of Congress Cataloging-in-Publication Data:
Milliron, Kerry.
Queen of the Amazons / by Kerry Milliron p. cm. — "Based on the Universal television series created by John Schulian and Robert Tapert ; adapted from the episode 'Hooves and harlots,' teleplay by Steven L. Sears." Summary: Xena helps her friend Gabrielle thwart the plans of a scheming warlord to start a war between the Amazons and the Centaurs in order to gain control of Arborea. ISBN: 0-679-88296-0 [1. Amazons—Fiction. 2. Centaurs—Fiction. 3. Princesses—Fiction.] I. Title. II. Title: Xena, warrior princess PZ7.M63947Qu 1996 [E]—dc20 96-14179

Printed in the United States of America 10 9 8 7 6 5 4 3 2 1

Random House 🏠 New York

In a time of ancient gods, warlords, and kings, a land in turmoil cried out for a hero. She was Xena, a mighty princess forged in the heat of battle. Her courage would change the world.

Xena once commanded vast armies, spreading terror, pain, and suffering. But the noble Hercules changed Xena's heart—and she joined the fight against evil.

With her best friend, Gabrielle, Xena traveled the land and fought for peace, wherever it was threatened.

Their journeys led them to Arborea,
a land in desperate need of their help.
Arborea was divided between
two civilizations: the Amazons and the
Centaurs. The Amazons were a powerful
group of warrior women, unusually
strong and highly skilled in battle.

The Centaurs were creatures that were half-man, half-horse—a gentle, noble race who turned to violence only as a last resort.

The Amazons and the Centaurs never trusted each other, because they were so different.

As the two heroines passed through the Arborean forest, Gabrielle chattered excitedly. "I've never seen an Amazon or a Centaur. Do you think we'll meet any?"

"Maybe sooner than you'd think." Xena eyed the treetops warily. Someone was watching them.

Suddenly, a hail of arrows flew past Xena and Gabrielle, and a young woman fell from the treetops. Gabrielle rushed to protect the stranger with her own body.

"I am the Amazon princess, Terreis," the dying woman gasped. "Only an Amazon warrior would act the way you did. I give you my birthright. From this day forward, you are princess of the Amazons."

A band of Amazon warriors descended slowly from the treetops. They wore eerie masks and were armed for battle.

"We were patrolling our border when the ambush came. It must have been the Centaurs. Come, we will take you to the Amazon queen."

At the Amazon camp, word of the princess's death had already arrived. Funeral drums boomed to mourn the loss of a great warrior, and the Amazons bowed to their new princess, Gabrielle.

In the middle of the ceremony, a group of Amazons burst into camp, dragging a Centaur in shackles.

"He was trying to escape across the river," shouted one of the Amazons. "His arrows are a perfect match for the one that killed Princess Terreis!"

The queen of the Amazons stepped forward and ordered, "Lock him up! He will be executed at noon tomorrow...by the new princess." She glared at Gabrielle. "We will see if you are worthy of my daughter's birthright."

The young Centaur
was Phantes, son of Tyldus,
king of the Centaurs.

Phantes' father was a
powerful leader.
Xena's army had once faced
his Centaurs in battle
but neither side had won.
The execution of Phantes
would surely send Tyldus
to war against the Amazons.

"I don't think I can go through with this," Gabrielle told Xena. "I can't just kill another...person, even if he is only half-human."

"You won't have to," Xena assured her. "I don't believe Phantes murdered Terreis. Centaurs are known for their sense of honor. I'm going to talk to Phantes myself."

In the Amazon prison, Xena questioned Phantes.

"On the name of my father," Phantes swore, "I didn't kill the Amazon woman. The real killer is the warlord Krykus. He wants the Amazons and Centaurs to wipe each other out. Then he'll have all of Arborea for himself."

Xena set off at once for Krykus' camp.

The sentry at **Krykus'** headquarters tried to stop Xena, but he was no match for the warrior princess. A few quick punches, and he was out like a light. Now she just had to find some evidence that Krykus was the real murderer.

Back at the Amazon camp, the queen handed Gabrielle her sword. It was time for Phantes' execution. "Kill the murderer!" she ordered.

Gabrielle did not know what to do. Luckily, Xena arrived just in time. "I have proof that Phantes is *not* the murderer!" Xena called out.

"I found Centaur arrows hidden in Krykus' camp. He used them to frame Phantes and start a war between the Amazons and the Centaurs."

Blinded by grief for her daughter, the Amazon queen cried, "This proves nothing. The execution will commence!"

There was only one way to stop the execution—a fight to the death with the queen of the Amazons.

"I demand the Royal Challenge!" Xena shouted.

"Then prepare to die," replied the queen, striking Xena with her fighting sticks.

Xena blocked the fierce blows of the Amazon queen, then leaped and spun to avoid being killed. With a diving roll, she took the queen by surprise and pinned her to the ground.

"Don't fight me to the death," Xena begged. "I need you to help stop this war."

In her heart, the queen knew that Xena was right. She called off the execution. Together, she and Xena said a final good-bye to Princess Terreis.

With Phantes free and Krykus' plot exposed, the Amazons and the Centaurs joined forces. Both armies confronted the scheming warlord. "I guess I'll have to take Arborea the old-fashioned way...by force!" threatened Krykus.

"Take your best shot," Xena replied.

The battle was soon over. Krykus and his men were easily defeated and driven off.

Thanks to Xena, peace prevailed once more in Arborea.

"I just thought of something," Gabrielle giggled as they rode off in search of new adventures. "You're a warrior princess, and now I'm an Amazon princess! This is going to make a *great* story."